LEFT BEHIND

a demigods story

HARRIET WADHAM

Edited by Corinna Downes
Cover by Lily Wadham
Typeset by Jonathan Downes,
Cover and Layout by SPiderKaT for CFZ Communications
Using Microsoft Word 2000, Microsoft , Publisher 2000, Adobe Photoshop CS.

First published in Great Britain by Fortean Fiction

CFZ Press Group
Myrtle Cottage
Woolsery
Bideford
North Devon
EX39 5QR

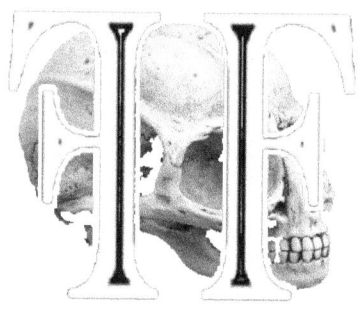

ISBN: 978-1-905723-64-5

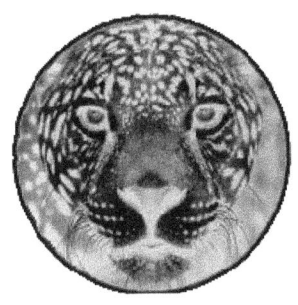

AUTHOR'S NOTE

Hello; it's the author here.

I just wanted to put in this note because of all the encouragement and support I've received during the writing of this book: To my parents, for getting me to read to them every single night when I was a little girl. To all my friends for making up these characters and giving me their permission to use them. Finally, to my boyfriend. I love you very much and I'm just so glad that one day, sitting in your garden, we decided to make up two superheroes - Jaguar and Psychic.

No, the idea of Jaguar wasn't taken from a popular comic book character.

Not at all.

I'll also definitely thank *Metallica*, *The Birthday Massacre* and *Skillet* for all your music! You've inspired me so much in my writing. There are plenty of other music artists that have aided me along my way, but I won't have room to mention them here. Lastly, thank you ever so much to Jon and the CFZ, for publishing this for me. It was my life's dream to be published.

I love you all ever such a lot.

Harriet.

Eclipse belongs to: M. Griffin
Arrow: S. Newell
Psychic: D. Bates
*UltraViole*t: O. Marsh
Miss Attitude: E. Raja
Force Girl: E. Milum
Phoenix: M. Sturmey
Hyper: R. Fox
Flashe: K. Garford
Atom: C. Hunt
Flex: K. Garford
Maimai: O. Marsh
Shout and Shove: C. Hunt and J. Tate
Stars: J. Tate
Sense: C. Cousins
The SunGod Corporation: O. Marsh
Myriad Blue: L. Wadham
Bugman: N. Wadham
Jack/Seven: M. Griffin and I

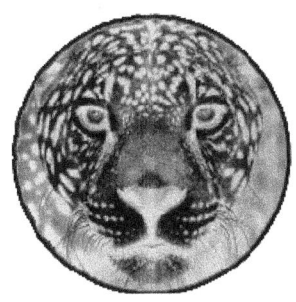

CHAPTER ONE

The battlefield was littered with corpses.

Phoenix ducked and dodged, blasting light at every opponent who stood in her way. An armed soldier leapt up in front of her and she immediately increased the heat in his body. Just to make it look good, right before he exploded, Phoenix pushed a great big fireball into his face, which ignited on the oils in his skin, making him appear as if he'd spontaneously combusted.

The numbers of the soldiers had decreased dramatically and it was looking like the four of them (Eclipse, Jaguar, Psychic and Phoenix) were winning. Psychic was blasting off soldiers into the distance, Eclipse was throwing them, swiping at them and stabbing them.

Jaguar was... was there any other way to say it? Well...

Jaguar was inherently brutal. Stab, roll, kick, punch and everything in-between. Phoenix flung off a couple of fireballs at a group of soldiers and they went burning down to hell.

The fighting carried on for about ten minutes, until Phoenix suddenly screamed at everyone with 'GET BEHIND ME!' They scrambled out of the way: Phoenix yelled a wordless yell, sweeping her arms out in front of her in an arc of fire and light and heat, frying the fighters like fritters. Eclipse looked at her, her head cocked at an angle.

'I think we're done,' she said.

'I could have taken them all on - and won.' Jaguar muttered grumpily. Always one for a brawl.

Psychic simply said, 'To be blunt, I don't see the point.'

'What....' Phoenix began, spinning around. She stopped.

'Well, I do,' Eclipse murmured.

Jaguar jumped around and immediately noticed the end of the sword sticking out from Psychic's chest.

'To be blunt? See the point? Geddit?' Psychic choked out, and collapsed to the ground.

Jaguar screamed in wrath and launched herself at the soldier who'd stabbed Psychic.

It took five seconds for her to drastically reduce his overwhelming mass to tatters, ribbons and blood.

They leapt to Psychic's side, except for Eclipse, who quietly looked on. Phoenix decided her friend didn't know what to say.

Jaguar cradled his head in her lap, tears already trickling down her cheeks.

'Look... I'm not dead yet...,' Psychic managed to say, fighting against the coughs that were threatening to rip his life from him.

'Take my healing power then. Do it! Please, Psy, heal..."

'Guys...,' Eclipse started; then closed her mouth. Phoenix looked at her with panicked eyes, pleading for her help.

Phoenix heard Psychic trying to say something.

Jaguar moaned for him to try to heal himself again.

And he said he couldn't.

Phoenix knew they were all lost then.

'It won't work, Jaguar. The sword... I think it had poison on it - can't-be-sure....,'

Blood bubbled up through his lips and Jaguar wiped it away.

'Try.'

'I have...'

'Try harder! You *can't leave me!*' She spurted out in frustration.

Psychic, despite his oncoming doom, gave her a smile that dazzled even Phoenix. He spoke again, for the last time.

'We'll meet again, someday. Some place better than here...'

Psychic choked. Ultimately, his eyes closed and the breath left his body.

Phoenix would later on try to push the memory of Jaguar sobbing over her fiancé's body out of her mind, but in vain. Jaguar crooned something unintelligible; however, try as they might, neither Phoenix nor Eclipse could pick it up.

Eclipse, shaking her head, began to trudge away.

Phoenix, devastated, followed her.

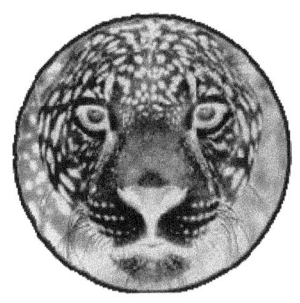

CHAPTER TWO

O ne day had passed without the existence of Psychic, and Jaguar was already near suicidal. She moped about the place like the world had gone to ruin. Whenever Phoenix or Eclipse attempted to engage her in conversation, she shrugged, didn't answer, or smiled a very sad smile.

Phoenix felt like Jaguar's depression was infecting them all. She knew from experience that Eclipse already had problems, but the recent events had affected her tall friend in ways both spiritually and mentally.

Eclipse looked out of the picturesque arched window. Night was falling. Her defined vision allowed her to already note the light of one star prying through the veil of day-light. She shrugged and put down the book she was reading: *Skulduggery Pleasant - Death Bringer*. Eclipse strode past Jaguar, who had her knees tucked up under her chin and was staring off into space. She strode into the corridor, walked the fairly long distance to the room she and Phoenix shared, and closed the door.

Eclipse didn't hear anybody moving.

She went back to the door, opened it, and closed it again.

Still nothing.

In a fit of anger, she slammed the door shut as hard as she could, and with a creak and a splinter, it fell off its hinges.

We'll have to get Psychic to fix that - Eclipse thought; then stopped herself; but it was too late. Psychic had always hated it when Eclipse busted the doors. It had meant he had to actually *move* to fix it.

A thought occurred that instantly clicked in Eclipse's crazy mind. Bust all the doors! He wasn't around anymore, so why not!

No. Eclipse could almost hear Psychic's telepathic thought in her head, warning her not to do this!

Eclipse's eyes narrowed. *Wait a second...*

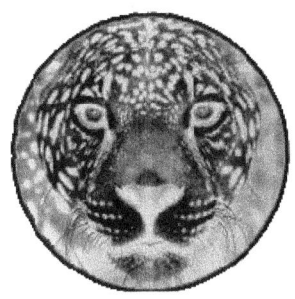

CHAPTER THREE

J aguar heard the door fall off its hinges. She thought about going over to try to help, but decided against it. Jaguar waited a little bit more; she lost track of time a bit, but who cared?

Eventually, Jaguar heaved her weary metal bones to her bedroom. She heard Eclipse call to her in a frenzied tone. She ignored it. Eclipse could fix her own bloody doors. Not Jaguar's problem at all. Jaguar pushed open the door to her bedroom. She had to think of it that way now - *her* bedroom, not her and….

Jaguar inwardly yelled at herself to *shut the hell up*. She pulled off her clothes and tugged a nightie over her body. It was red, and she herself had stitched the J on to the bottom of it, near her left leg. She then slid a dressing gown over it, but not hers. The silky smooth silver satin felt nice on her skin, and she rubbed her face in it.

A tear trickled down her pale cheek and splashed on the satin. She knew it would leave a mark.

~o0o~

Phoenix didn't sleep in the same room as Eclipse that night. She didn't feel safe enough, not with her room-mate in that state. For God's sake, she had just broken the door!

Of course, nobody else was able to fix that. Jaguar probably could, but wouldn't. Phoenix didn't have the DIY know-how, and Eclipse just wouldn't. Instead, Phoenix slept in the spare bedroom that night. She pulled back the blue bedcovers, lay down on the bed and snuggled up in her *Betty Boop* pyjamas.

She lay there for a bit and thought about the previous day's events. How she had lost a friend, and, on the following day, lost two more.

~oOo~

Understandably, Jaguar had found it partially impossible to go to sleep. So, she decided, she would go out on the balcony. Her pale feet padded along the hallway. She found some slippers and slid them on her feet. Jaguar trotted down a wide flight of stairs, turned left and pushed aside the sliding door that led out to the balcony. A soft, meandering breeze played around with her hair. It brought back calming childhood memories. She stepped out onto the tiled balcony, and placed her hands on the railings. This was the second most calming place for her in the world.

The first, however, no longer existed.

Footsteps. Behind her.

Jaguar knew she was asleep and dreaming.

A familiar scent. A hand slipped over hers, soft and warm.

'You're dead, you know,' she murmured.

'And why aren't you panicking?'

'Because I'm dreaming.'

'Your logic is sound.'

Jaguar chuckled, and leaned against him. He did feel very real, but she knew dreams did. Psychic kissed the top of her head, and she tilted her head up to see him better.

'This is so clichéd,' she muttered and he laughed as well.

'I think this is the last time I'll see you. Properly,' Jaguar continued. 'My dad used to tell me that when we're asleep, our souls wander from our bodies and discover places. If another person you know is in your dream, your souls have met.' She wrinkled up her nose. 'Or it might be spirits. I can't remember.'

Psychic stroked her arm, making small shivers of tranquillity flow up and down her spine.

'You know…,' he began, 'there was one more thing. I was going to tell you about it before I died, but… there you go.'

'Tell me now,' she begged.

'You may not like it,' Psychic warned her.

'Me? Not liking something you're telling me? Psychic, I thought you knew me better than that…'

Psychic smiled and bent down to whisper to her, though there was nobody else about. Her eyes widened.

'Ah. *That* one more thing,' she whispered. Psychic took her other hand in his, and she grinned up at him, her eyes sparkling with joy.

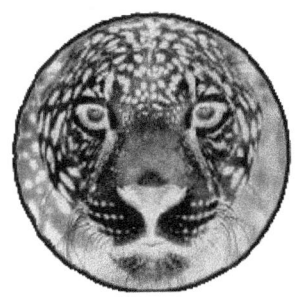

CHAPTER FOUR

T he morning sun managed to find a way to get into the room, even though the curtains were shut tight. It seeped round the edges with gentle tendrils of yellow.

Eclipse stirred. She didn't *want* to wake up! She still couldn't be bothered.

But she had to, seeing as she had to fix the door.

The door.

She opened her bleary eyes to find that the door was back in its normal place.

The door!

Eclipse leaped out of bed, tripped on the bedcovers, rolled and came up in a crouch. She straightened a bit, then tiptoed forwards and sniffed the door. There were traces of a certain scent. She peeked into the gap between the doorframe and the door itself.

Yes, there was an extremely faint blue glow…

'PHOENIX! JAGUAR!' She bellowed, as loud as she could!

~o0o~

Phoenix sat bolt upright in bed, expected to hit her head on the ceiling, and then realised she wasn't on the bunk-bed.

Thankfully.

Her eyes were still closed. Eclipse, from somewhere upstairs, yelled her name. Phoenix sighed. She didn't really want to go upstairs, but then, it was better to. Who knew what random path Eclipse would take?

She finally opened her eyes, letting the light infiltrate them. It felt good.

Phoenix screamed.

It wasn't possible, what she was seeing here wasn't possible but it was happening right there!

~o0o~

Jaguar rolled over to face him.

He wasn't there. She sighed; it had just been a dream. No Psychic. No kisses.

No cuddles.

She told herself to stop being silly. She knew she couldn't get over him: she knew she wouldn't allow herself to, either. Dejected, she breathed in through her nose, then out through her mouth. Calming technique. She had learned it from her traumatic days during biology, that time she had to have her moulds done when she was 12, when she had her Tetanus jabs.

In through the nose, out through the mouth. In through the nose....

No way, it couldn't be possible.

She gathered the sheets up on Psychic's side of the bed and breathed in deeply.

His scent. Fresh from one hour ago. She sniffed again - she was right. Jaguar turned her attention to the pillow and scrutinised it hard. There. She plucked out a couple of hairs between her finger and thumb. They were blonde, short (ish), and fresh.

She had to get to Flashe.

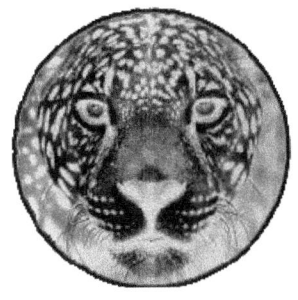

CHAPTER FIVE

Eclipse called again, after hearing Phoenix's scream. She leapt and in midair her most prominent power kicked in. Her legs lengthened and grew sandy fur, while her clothes sank into her skin. It was all painless. As she landed gracefully on all four paws, shaking her shaggy head, Eclipse had transformed into a grand lioness. A blue diamond was sunk into the flesh in her left-hand (or left-paw) side, but her eyes stayed the same colours- red on the left, blue on the right. It was an entrancing case of complete Heterochromia. The clothes she was wearing, though they were absorbed in her skin, mainly lent their colour to her nose. As she had previously been wearing blue pyjamas, her nose was a subtle shade of blue. Her paws thudded down the stairs to Phoenix's room and once she was there she transformed back into a human, gaining all of her clothing and her standard appearance once again. Phoenix was sat on the bed, looking pale as a sheet.

'Phoenix, what's up? You look like you've seen a ghost!' Eclipse panted.

'I think I just have.' Phoenix rasped. She pointed out of the window. Eclipse raced to it.

'What?' She queried. 'There's nothing out there.' She heard Phoenix getting up from behind her. Phoenix cautiously approached the window.

'Eclipse... I think I just saw Psychic...' Phoenix mumbled.

'That's funny, because he just fixed our bedroom door.' Eclipse informed her, her red and blue eyes locking on Phoenix's panicked brown eyes. Phoenix's eyebrows shot up.

~o0o~

Jaguar was dressed, once again, in her leathers. She wore a determined expression on her face; a woman fixing to perform a very dangerous task. She pushed the front doors open and strode over to the garage. She pressed the button on the garage keys; instantaneously, the door slid open, with a creak and a groan.

Parked in the middle of the out-building was her old red quad bike. She remembered looting it from ASIMOV, back when they were beginners. Scared, anxious and completely untrained.

The past, however, was now behind them. Jaguar remembered replacing the hubcaps with the ASIMOV logo with ones that bore the Demigods logo. Fun times indeed.

She hopped on and turned a key in the ignition. It started up like a dream. Jaguar grinned, revved the engine and zoomed off, in the direction of the house that her two friends, Flashe and Flex, shared. The hair samples were tucked neatly in her pocket. Jaguar knew that Flashe, being a doctor, could analyse them.

~o0o~

Phoenix ran up to Jaguar's room, but she wasn't in there. She panicked, looking left to right. Instinctively, she raced back down, coming face to face with Eclipse.

'Eclipse! She's not there! How are we going to tell her about Psychic?' Phoenix panicked.

'I think she already knows. Look.' Eclipse told her, pointing out the window. Phoenix could see, in the far distance, Jaguar tearing down the road on her quad bike, fully dressed.

Nodding, Phoenix heaved a very big sigh of relief.

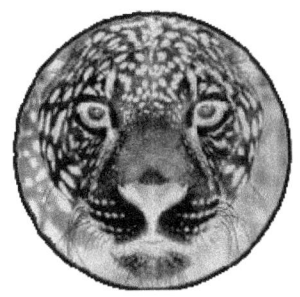

CHAPTER SIX

F lashe had just sat down to her breakfast when there came a curious rapping on the door.

There's only one person who'd be here this early. She reflected, expecting the worst. Flashe heaved herself over to the front door and opened it.

To her immense surprise, it wasn't Atom attempting to use the quarter of a brain that she possessed.

'Jaguar? What are *you* doing here?' Flashe asked, astounded.

'I need you to analyse these hair samples. Tell me how old they are, how long they've been detached from the head.'

Flashe blinked. 'Jaguar, Psychic's dead.'

'I have reason to believe that he's not.'

'The lab's upstairs, second door to the left.'

~o0o~

Flex rubbed his eyes. It was only half eight, for goodness' sake, and already one of Flashe's friends had come round. He had been looking forward to a nice lie-in, too.

Never mind.

He stretched his flexible arm around the bedpost and hauled himself up. Flex extended his arm out, pulled open the drawer and patted about in there until he found a clean pair of jeans.

Eventually, after getting dressed, he trudged along the hall to the lab, where he knew he could find Flashe and... which one was it? Eclipse or Jaguar? He always got them mixed up; even though they had an extremely drastic distance in height, they were both so alike in their vindictive ways.

Flex pushed open the lab door, immediately arousing hushed shushes from the girls. He saw them bent over a microscope, both focusing their complete concentration on something laid out on a slide. He walked over for a closer view, puzzling as to what it could be. Suddenly, Flashe jotted something down on a notepad she was carrying. He couldn't read it.

Flashe jerked away, catching Flex by surprise. Her eyes weren't focused, meaning only one thing.

Flashe was having a vision.

Jaguar seemed to notice it too. She sat there expectantly, evidently not knowing what she was supposed to do. However, Flex did; he jumped round to face Flashe's face, came level with her, and held her hand. He jerked his head towards Flashe, meaning for Jaguar to come over and do the same. She did so.

~o0o~

Jaguar hunkered down in front of Flashe, and, like Flex, gripped one of her hands. Instantly, the Vision began, almost as if the floor had been ripped out from underneath her. It was herself, screaming in agony.

What; am I getting tortured or someth....

Be quiet.

She heard Flex tell her.

Jaguar decided, just this once, to obey him without killing him.

It cut to another vision of her again, her back turned to the angle the Vision was letting her view from. Jaguar could see she was smiling, rocking something in her arms. The door opened and Psychic walked in! Jaguar's heart soared. He was alive! He walked over to Vision-Jaguar and gave her a kiss on the cheek.

Vision-Jaguar turned around and out of the million things she could have had in her arms it was a baby.

Jaguar felt her mouth drop and go dry, even though she couldn't actually see it, which was weird. Vision-Jaguar walked over to a cradle and gently placed the baby in it, cooing softly. There were two other cradles in the room, with babies in! Vision-Psychic placed his hand on her waist and she leaned into him, adoringly.

The Vision ended.

'I'M HAVING CHILDREN?!' Jaguar screeched.

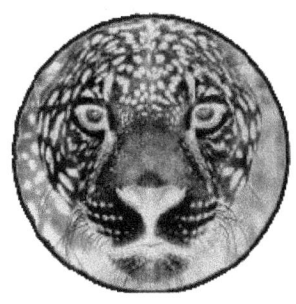

CHAPTER SEVEN

It had been a week since the surprising Vision. Jaguar eased her foot down on the brake and pulled the handbrake. She opened the car door, eager to escape from the confines of the black car she'd rented for the funeral. Her black mini-dress clung to her sweaty figure. Nervously, Jaguar pushed open the door to the church.

Everyone was seated in the pews.

Jaguar had chosen this place for the funeral, not because she was Christian (indeed, she wouldn't ever have been able to find religion in herself even if she tried), but because it was easy to address the crowd. Striding past the rows of people, she could have named just about everyone in the audience. Arrow, Flashe, Maimai, UltraViolet, Atom (even her young cousins Shout and Shove), Ki… She needed them here, now.

Only Flashe and Flex knew what was coming, though. Jaguar stepped up to the altar and, clearing her throat, began a shaky speech.

'You've all come here to celebrate the life of a great man. However, all is not as it seems.' She glanced back at the coffin, a metre behind her. Her heart thudded and thundered.

'He wouldn't have wanted you to mourn his death. Partly because he lived life to the full…' Jaguar walked behind the coffin and stroked her hand across its smooth, mahogany surface. 'And partly because he would have felt you were expecting him to die or something.' With a grin slightly turning up the corner of her mouth, she pulled open the coffin lid.

For a split second everybody thought she had gone quite insane. Then somebody shouted, '*Look!*' and they did.

Gasps rippled through the crowd. Eclipse nudged Arrow, who had nodded off a bit.

As soon as he opened his eyes he yelped. 'But I thought..'

'We all did, idiot,' Eclipse muttered.

'I need your help. We all now know he is alive somewhere. If you don't believe me, ask Flashe. But I'll be requesting the assistance of the geographically inclined masses to plot courses. I'll need those of you with friends in high places to get on the 'phone. Most of all...'

Here Jaguar faltered, looking about the church, scanning their bewildered faces.

She cleared her throat. 'Most of all, I'll need hope. From the lot of you, because if we haven't even at least got hope then it'll all fail. I'm not ordering you to do this. A lot of you won't want to.' Jaguar shot a look at Stars, who fidgeted uncomfortably.

'The only reason I can't do this alone is because... well...,' Jaguar breathed in a bit, and then continued with:

'I think I'm having triplets.'

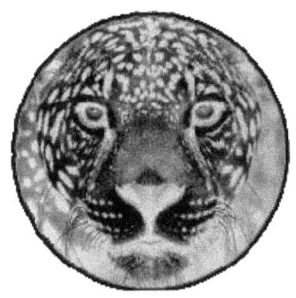

CHAPTER EIGHT

J aguar hoped that the little pep talk she'd given at the church should have been enough to rally enthusiasm among the numbers.

However, she was terrified. Terrified that her pregnancy wouldn't go smoothly, that the unborn triplets wouldn't even make it to their first wail. She wasn't particularly enthusiastic about having children; they would be a distraction, and would also be in jeopardy all the time. Having superheroes for parents wouldn't be safe, she knew that. Jaguar could practically sense Eclipse's eagerness to babysit, but could find none within herself.

Slowly, the weeks dragged themselves by, like sluggish, sleepy snails. Surprisingly, there weren't that many helpers from the Demigods' side. Arrow had been dying to help, so Jaguar had set him to work plotting courses. She remembered the talk they'd had at the church.

'You're having triplets?'

'Um… yes,' Jaguar had confirmed reluctantly.

'You're *pregnant?*' Arrow had persisted. Somehow, Jaguar hadn't liked the sound of that phrase.

'For want of a better word… yeah,' she'd told him grumpily.

'Can I babysit?' Arrow had asked, bright eyed and bushy-tailed.

'No, Arrow. The kids would probably want to shoot each other with the weapon.'

'What if I left it at home?'

'Arrow, you *never* go anywhere without your bow.' Jaguar had then snapped.

Luckily, Arrow had seen sagacity in this and his puppy-dog impersonation disappeared.

Stars had predictably bailed out, not wanting to get her 'pretty' hands dirty. Atom, surprisingly, had made up for this by bringing along a good friend of hers, Sense. Sense was Canadian and Jaguar respected her from the start. Sense had helped the plan go efficiently from the moment Jaguar had said, 'That's it, I guess.'

The presence of the babies was making itself felt in the Demigods household already. Phoenix had been seen dressing up one of the spare bedrooms and going out to Argos with a purse stuffed with cash. She had been just about to walk out of the front door when Jaguar had caught her softly by the arm and said, 'Don't.'

Jaguar, however, was in a spot of bother. There still weren't enough helpers; they had to search the globe. Jaguar knew that Psychic would try to hide from them, to get his affairs in order. She was also worried about Eclipse. She hadn't seen her tall friend for a while now, and felt she needed her for moral support.

Eventually, she picked up the 'phone and dialled Force Girl's number.

Force Girl answered on the third ring. 'Hello?'

'It's Jaguar. FG, I'm tired and we haven't got enough helpers.'

'So what you're basically saying is… you need my help?'

'Yes,' Jaguar admitted miserably. She didn't usually try to get other people's help, even though she had said she needed it in front of 30 or more superheroes.

'Well… do you know anybody with lots of associates, who can help us with this predicament? I do.'

Jaguar thought hard for a moment. 'Um… No. Sorry…actually, there's the SunGod Corporation.'

'They don't help people with affairs like this, they just study us.'

'Damn. Well, I'm stuck for ideas.'

'I'm not.' Force Girl told her. Jaguar momentarily pondered if Force Girl knew something she didn't, until she latched onto the notion.

'Oh, no.' Jaguar seethed.

'It's the only way,' Force Girl told her, sadly.

Jaguar felt more frustrated than she ever had in her life. 'I'm going to have to think about that one. Goddammit, I hope Psychic knows what I'm going through to get him back. Thanks... I think.'

Jaguar put down the phone. Butterflies were fluttering about in her stomach, and alarm bells were ringing in her ears. Every instinct she possessed was screaming at her to not do it, to say 'We can do this on our own.'

However, she felt she had no choice.

Everyone's going to hate you. Her conscience informed her.

Shut the hell up. She told herself, transitorily expecting to have gone quite insane.

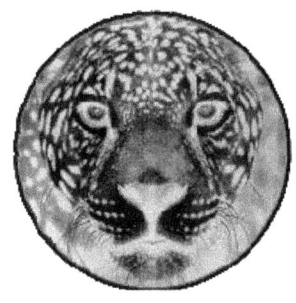

CHAPTER NINE

U nderstandably, Atom was happy in her work. Saving people every day! She didn't have to be clever for *that*, did she? Well, sometimes, but she could always rely on Force Girl or UltraViolet for a plan, or direchuns.

When Jag had asked her for help, Atom had decided to be a nice person and voluntarily volunteer. (She was happy she knew those two words, and liked to put them together as often as she could.)

Voluntarily volunteering, Atom had bounced up to Jaggy and said 'Oooh, ooh, I'll do it! I wanna help!' Jaggy had immediately told her to patrol the house. Atom felt really, really happy and was now pacing in circles around the nice biggy house that Clipsy, Jaggy and Pheenicks and Sicic owned.

Atom frowned. Nothing was happening. There wasn't anyone there! This thought was immediately dispelled when she saw a cloaked figure she didn't know walking on the path in front of the house. She bounded over.

''Scoose me, who are you? I don't know you but I'm goading the house in case of evil peoples.' Atom waved her fingers about at the 'evil peoples' bit and tried her best to put on a spooky voice.

As it was, the person looked a bit worried for Atom's mental wellbeing.

A realisation struck Atom like a bowl of cheese. 'I saw you at the big pretty building! You were the one talking to Jaggy Waggy and looking like a squirrel!'

'Yeah, I'm Arrow. You do know she hates to be called 'Jaggy Waggy'?' Arrow informed her.

'I know, but I can't remember her proper name.' Atom smiled, wanly. 'Well, as long as you don't hurt anyone I think you can go in! Byee!' She skipped away, overjoyed that she was doing such a good job of her voluntary volunteering.

~o0o~

Arrow had decided to be rid of the strange girl in red as soon as possible, so he quickly jogged into the house. Jaguar was in the living room, looking like death warmed up.

'Jaguar, you do realise that your guard is a simpleton on a stick?'

'Yeah, that's why she's patrolling the house. I think I'm going to notice a bad guy myself when I see one. Anyway, Atom's not doing any harm.'

'It annoys me just as much as it annoys you when she calls you 'Jaggy Waggy'.'

'I have told her multiple times to call me Jaguar.'

'She can't remember that.'

'Maybe I should yell it in her face a couple of times.'

Suddenly, they both heard a scream from outside, and raced to the window. However, it was only Atom, jumping up and down with excitement as she pointed at an unfortunate cat that had managed to prance into the garden. Arrow felt sorry for the poor thing as Atom began chasing it in 3-year-old excitement.

'Why is she so thick?' Arrow groaned.

'Every time she regenerates she loses a huge chunk of her IQ. As it is, we estimate it's down to about minus a million right now,' Jaguar told him, matter-of-factly.

Arrow nodded, wisely. He then turned his attention to more important matters. 'Jaguar, I saw how you looked just then. I know we don't have enough helpers, and...I don't know what to do.'

Jaguar looked like she wanted to slit her own throat. 'I've been advised to take drastic measures.'

'Such as?'

Arrow watched her take a deep breath. Then another one.

'We're going to have to turn to people we've never expected help from.'

Arrow blinked.

'For God's sake, Arrow, we have to turn to ASIMOV.'

Arrow promptly fainted.

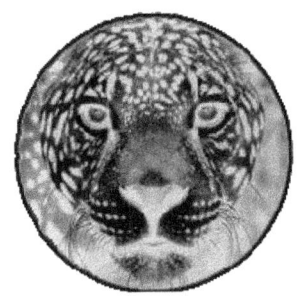

CHAPTER TEN

I seated myself in the chair. It wasn't too comfy, but I wouldn't be here for very long.

Another woman walked into the room. 'Ah, you've arrived, then.'

'Well done. I'm considering taking you up on your offer,' I said. My heart was thumping hard in my chest, like a caged animal attempting to squeeze through my ribcage.

The other one nodded, pleased with both her and me. Her eyes locked on my own. I stared back, keeping up the façade of determination.

She said, 'To tell the truth, I doubted you would even consider it.' I raised an eyebrow.

'That's not very reassuring,' I said.

'You do realise,' she said, placing her massive bulk in a chair opposite me, 'that if they manage to get him back your secrets won't be very safe?'

I smirked. 'You do realise that you need to join a gym?'

'What?'

'Never mind, anyway. I'm going to go to the SunGod Corporation for a telepathic shield. It'll freak him out a bit, but when he can be bothered, he'll come to a conclusion that it's something natural. Also, I want to tell you something.'

'What would you like to tell me?'

I braced myself. I was betraying her, betraying my friend, betraying the Demigods, but I couldn't ignore my natural instincts for much longer.

'Jaguar's expecting triplets,' I finally managed to blurt out.

The only light in the room was a single candle. Its flame flickered, illuminating her face.

'We know that. However, you have just proved your efficiency in providing information. I thank you for your time,' she told me.

I still couldn't ignore the pain I was feeling. 'So, what now?'

She smiled a sickly leer, and even in the dim light I could point out the gaps in between her remaining yellow teeth. 'Welcome to the team.'

I took her outstretched hand and shook it, feeling the burden on my back getting ever weightier.

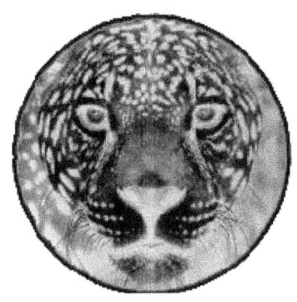

CHAPTER ELEVEN

Force Girl, tell me... Do you think Jaguar's a virgin?' UltraViolet asked Force Girl, who was exerting herself over the work she was doing.

'Well, of course not. When a woman's pregnant, she *isn't* a virgin. Anyway, it's not polite to be discussing our friend's virginity', Force Girl snapped, surprised that UltraViolet could even say a thing as irrational as that. She heaved the object shut. It sprang open again and she growled in angst.

UV hung her head. 'You're right. Sorry.'

'It's not me you should be apologising to,' Force Girl muttered, and with a grunt, she finally managed to close her suitcase. UV was sat nonchalantly on her purple suitcase, looking at Force Girl.

Force Girl managed to catch her eye and they both ended up in fits of laughter.

'But seriously,' UV began, when they had ended their giggle-fest, 'Do you really think her and Psychic... um...,' she trailed off, not sure how to end the sentence.

'Jaguar's mostly responsible. She wouldn't do a thing like that without knowing the outcome,' Force Girl told UltraViolet.

UV frowned. 'But it'd be dangerous for her triplets. They might even get captured by ASIMOV, and who knows what could happen then?'

'I'm sure that she and Psychic would find a way to take care of the kids,' Force Girl assured her friend.

'I don't even think Psychic's alive,' UV sighed. 'I mean, Flashe claims they have evidence of his survival, but just an empty coffin doesn't prove it all, does it?'

'I think it's worth the effort. If he *was* alive, then he wouldn't be very reassured if we just left him to fend for himself in some other place.'

'You speak of him as if he was a baby...'

'Well, sometimes, I've noticed Psychic to be a little silly. You know, all that "I can't be *bothered*" stuff, and the "It takes too much *effort*" stuff.'

'Mm,' UV hmmed. She felt a little worried as to how this whole occurrence would unfold.

~o0o~

Speedily, she coasted on the air, leaving fiery trails. People would look up at her and gasp. She felt a little annoyed at them sometimes. She wasn't the only superhero in the area, was she? There were others, even besides the Demigods.

Only problem was, most of them tended to join ASIMOV, just for a chance to raise Cain. Miss Attitude despised supers like that - who used their powers purely to show off and make themselves look good. It never worked, anyway. It was usually a case of a tale that wasn't right.

She scanned the scenery below for the house that her affiliates, the Demigods, owned. Some of them didn't live there, but were still part of the big eight. She finally managed to spot it, and realised, with a sinking heart, that Atom was patrolling the grounds.

Well, ASIMOV wouldn't get in, *that* was for sure. Not.

She swooped down as fast as her pyrokinetic powers would enable her, startling Eclipse, who was just riding in on her blue motorbike. Allegedly, that bike was made from, or coated with, Lontoca, the very same metal that now encased Jaguar's bones in a shell of security. Eclipse parked the bike in the garage and, taking off her helmet, regarded Miss Attitude with something close to dislike.

'What are *you* doing here?' Eclipse asked. Miss Attitude knew why Eclipse was nervous around her. Eclipse disliked fire, though wild animals were usually drawn to it. Animals being frightened of fire was a bit of an urban myth.

'I've come to see you guys. I heard about Psychic's death/life thing, and decided to offer my services.'

'We already have a dragon.'

'What?'

Eclipse sighed and rolled her eyes. 'Fire, dragons? My god, you pyrokinetics can be …' She was interrupted by the pet idiot prancing around the corner.

'Ooh! You're Mrs Angrypants, aren't you! I'm Atom!' Atom trilled, dragging out the 'a' on the 'Atom'.

What. Is. This. Thing. Miss Attitude found herself thinking.

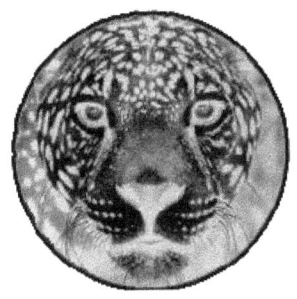

CHAPTER TWELVE

J aguar pelted out the back door. Miss Attitude, Eclipse and Atom were all outside, engaging in an awkward conversation in which Miss Attitude was trying to explain that she was *not* Mrs Angrypants, but Miss Attitude, or 'Tudie' for short. UV, having invisibly flown across, followed after her short friend. She wasn't used to following Jaguar, Jaguar never usually *had* a plan.

Jaguar stopped ahead of her and beckoned. UV, crouching low to avoid being spotted, silently shuffled closer.

'*We need to get to ASIMOV.*' Jaguar hissed to her.

'*I know; you told me already.*' UV whispered back. Jaguar looked forlorn at this, but quickly ran alongside her to her house. Once there, UV spread her arms wide and said grandly, 'Welcome to my humble abode!' UltraViolet had left her suitcase at the big house, but Jaguar needed her to drive her to ASIMOV tower.

UV didn't know why ASIMOV didn't move to a new location, even though the Demigods knew of their base of operations. She also didn't get why they couldn't go and demolish the tower someday.

She had been told repeatedly by Eclipse that it was because they didn't have the provisions, but UV knew better than that. After all, with the genius of Flashe on the team, who knew how far they could go?

UltraViolet opened the door for Jaguar, then closed it again behind herself. UV shared this house with Force Girl, though she was secretly considering moving out. She was getting a bit annoyed at her friend being on the 'phone all the time, or going out shopping with another person. It seemed to UV that she was just the spare tyre, only for use when all other ends had been explored and exhausted. So, UltraViolet had been glad when her friend had asked for help in tracking down Psychic.

Jaguar flopped down onto the sofa. 'God, I'm exhausted,' she grouched.

UV took a leap of faith. 'Jaguar, don't you think this is all a little... far-fetched?'

'What?'

'Well, you know... going to ask ASIMOV for help, when we only really have inconclusive evidence. I mean, who's to say that he really *is...*'

Jaguar pounced on her before she could finish. UltraViolet gasped in shock, unable to do anything else, being in such close proximity to those razor-sharp claws...

'Now you listen here, I *know* he's alive and we have all the evidence we *need*, you understand? If you don't like what we're about to do, then I'll just go back home and get on the quad bike,' Jaguar snarled. UltraViolet could feel the sadness rolling off her small friend in persistent waves.

'Yeah.. 'kay.' UV managed to squeak, and Jaguar rolled off her.

'Jeez, why did you have to do that?' UV cried, jumping up.

Jaguar looked up at her from her crouching position on the floor. 'Because if I don't have hope, then there's no way I'll find him.'

~o0o~

They had finally made it. UltraViolet saw Jaguar shield her eyes from the sun. They walked together towards the tall, intimidating tower. UV felt shivers roll over her skin. She still couldn't forget the torture she'd had to endure at the hands of these monsters. And now, they were asking them for *help*? It was insane!

Still, insanity was what Jaguar did best.

Immediately, several Jacks came pounding around the corner, fully armed with grenades, guns, knives and numerous other weapons that UV couldn't name.

'PUT YOUR HANDS BEHIND YOUR HEADS!' the leader called, monotonously.

The clones couldn't feel any pain or emotions, making them quite formidable. Flashe still hadn't managed to work out what they were made from.

UV exchanged looks with Jaguar, unsure as to what might come next.

Jaguar, unsurprisingly, didn't do as told. Instead she raised her palms in front of her in a calming gesture.

'I just want to talk to your leader, Ace.'

The bullets ripped through her instantaneously. She was flung backwards with the force of the metal hitting her. UV gasped; it was all she could manage to do.

Jaguar stayed splayed on the ground for a moment; then wearily got to her feet, dusting herself off. 'That's going to take *ages* to sew back up,' she moaned, gesturing to her red t-shirt. The Jacks stayed motionless, until Hades strode through the large doors of ASIMOV tower and waggled his eyebrows at them.

'Well *hello*, ladies. Have you realised just how *sexy* you both look today?' His eyes roved over to the very top of UV's dress, where it dipped in the middle with the sweetheart neckline.

She turned the glare factor up to 265.

He shrugged and ran a hand through his stupidly spiky hair. 'Seriously, what do you want?'

'We want to talk to Ace about stuff,' UV said.

'What kind of stuff?'

'Stuff that stupid boys like you don't understand.'

'I'm not a boy!'

'Stop acting like one then, you babyish brat. Now let us through, or we'll hurt you,' Jaguar interjected.

'You do realise that both your top and your bra are ripped in two?' UV hissed to Jaguar, sidling up next to her.

'That's why I didn't wear my *Metallica* top today,' Jaguar snarled, through gritted teeth.

'He can nearly see your ...'

Jaguar zipped up her jacket and whispered, 'How do you think we're actually going to *get* in?'

'I have no idea!' UV whispered down, urgently.

Jaguar stood there for a moment, her head bowed in thought. Her face suddenly seemed to light up with an idea. She instantly scowled, but began to walk forward slowly. The Jacks armed their rifles, but didn't shoot.

UV instantly realised where this was going. She saw Jaguar walk right up to Hades. She saw Hades sneak a look down the jacket. She saw Jaguar place her palm on the side of his face, lean in and then kick him in the balls.

As Hades screeched in agony, UV phased her particles through the ground, then *whooshed* back up through the slate floor of ASIMOV tower. She heard Jaguar pelt in behind her.

'Which way?' UV asked.

Jaguar sniffed the air, concentrated, then pelted up the stairs to their right. UV followed. Staircase after staircase lead them to the very top of the tower, which was a really silly place to have an office if you were despised globally.

Jaguar smashed open the door, to find Ace calmly perched (or was it splatted?) in her office chair.

'Y'all right?' Ace asked calmly.

'No, I'm not, and as stupid as this might sound, I need your bloody help.'

UV raised an eyebrow, still panting. *What an original approach.*

Ace was surprised. 'Why? What for?'

'Tracking down Psychic.'

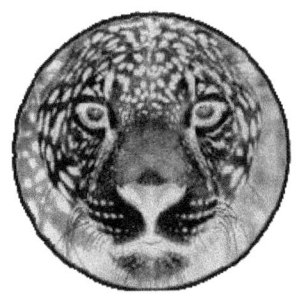

CHAPTER THIRTEEN

After the long, boring talk between herself, UV and Ace, Jaguar strode out of the tower, past Hades, who was still hopping around madly, glaring at them, and past the emotionless Jacks. She heard UV scurrying after her.

'You're grumpy,' UV told her.

'You think?' Jaguar snapped.

The journey home was uncomfortably silent. Jaguar was going to meet Ace and a few ASIMOVs at a far-off venue, which she'd already booked for the following week. It was a small hall, far enough for ASIMOV not to find out their location, but close enough for a trip that wouldn't take too long.

Jaguar collapsed on the front room sofa as soon as she got in. Her head was hurting and she still couldn't work out what Ace had been hinting at when she'd said, 'Life isn't easy for you, Jaguar. I reckon this is going to make it a lot harder…'

Ah well. She thought to herself, then trudged upstairs. She hadn't noticed how late it was getting. She passed under Eclipse, randomly curled up on the ceiling, dead to the world. Butterflies (or was it hornets?) were zooming around in her stomach, reminding her that every second wasted by eating, sleeping, waiting, was a second further away from finding her lover.

~o0o~

As the sun peeped over the horizon, Flashe rubbed her bleary eyes and noticed two things. First, Flex wasn't there. Second, she was in a strange room. Suddenly, the events of the previous four days came rushing back to her like an elastic band stretched to its limit. Psychic: Missing. Jaguar: Help! Flashe: Vision. Jaguar: Kids!

Flashe shook her head as she got up. Immediately, she got a head rush. She plonked down again on the bed as her head cleared, cautiously stood up again, and went downstairs for some breakfast. It had been a week (a very hectic week) since Jaguar and UV had returned from their little road trip. Flashe had asked where they'd been but to no avail. She had since contemplated using her power of visions, but had decided that it was best to let sleeping dogs lie.

Opening the cupboard, Flashe noticed a new carton of something. She picked it up and scrutinised it. Grape juice. A smile curved the corner of her mouth as she remembered those times Jaguar had come around when they'd been younger. She remembered her little brother hitting Jaguar with a pillow, a form of irritation that had come to be known as 'Pillow Torture.' Jaguar had been Hannah then, and Flashe had been Freya. Looking back, Flashe supposed that Freya *had* been a nice name, but still preferred her new name now.

Gently, arms encircled her from behind, making her lose her train of thought. She relaxed into Flex, happily acknowledging his presence.

'You've got a big day today,' Flex told her. Flashe recollected that they were all going out to this hall place to meet somebody, and she had been promised by Jaguar that she'd know all about who it was soon enough.

Flashe sighed and disentangled herself from his caring hold.

'I'm worried about what'll happen,' she confessed.

Flex took her hands in his. 'I'm sure Jaguar knows what she's doing. This all seems to have changed her. Maybe for the better? She might not be as reckless anymore.'

Flashe laughed. 'Oh, I'm sure after this has all blown over, she'll be the irritating midget that we all know and love.'

At that moment, Jaguar trudged into the kitchen, opened the cupboard, got out cereal, poured it into a bowl, got a spoon and some grape juice, glared at the two of them and trudged out again.

Flashe and Flex looked at each other.

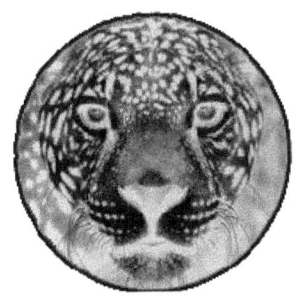

CHAPTER FOURTEEN

J aguar strode up to the big hall.

She noted that there were already many ASIMOV vehicles parked in the lot. Demigod transportation began to trickle in through the opening in the wall, making her feel comforted with the knowledge that she wouldn't be alone on this reckless grasp for aid.

As she walked around the corner, the sight of ASIMOV waiting at the back door, bickering among themselves, met her eyes. The chatter died down almost instantly; her eyes roamed over the group, recognising every single one of them. Inclining her head for them to follow, she walked round the front, fished rented keys out of her pocket and opened the door.

As she stood aside to let her enemies in, she noted with approval the size of the hall. There was already a large table set up in the middle, so they could discuss matters without having to come into contact.

Good. Jaguar decided.

Ace seated herself at the head of the table, while the rest of the Demigods and their numerous associates filtered through. A smile lit up Jaguar's face as she acknowledged the presence of Bugman, her dad. He caught her eye and grinned, while a tiger centipede wound itself lovingly round his wrist. Momentarily, Jaguar wondered how he'd managed to seduce it into being friendly; then decided that there were more important matters to discuss. Eventually, every hero and villain had arrived.

Now there was only one goal in her mind - to enlist their help and get Psychic back, fast. Sitting herself directly opposite from Ace, she looked her right in the eye.

First to speak. She thought.

'I really don't want to do this,' she began, before she was interrupted by a loud bashing on the door. Everyone slowly turned their heads to stare at the door, though Jaguar already knew who it was. Phoenix gracefully rose to get it. Standing in the doorway, fashionably late, was Myriad Blue, Jaguar's effortlessly irritating big sister. Phoenix scowled like her worst nightmare had come to life - Phoenix having powers of light, and Myriad having powers of darkness, the two clashed every time they met.

Myriad plonked down next to Jaguar, in poor Phoenix's seat. Phoenix's face became thunderous, but she chose to suppress it and sat somewhere else. Unfortunately, that was right next to Hades, who kept trying to look down her top. She continually had to burn his thigh.

Myriad yelled, 'I'M HERE!'

'Thank you. We've noticed.' Jaguar snarled, turning her pack-it-in glare up to 11. She continued.

'As I was *saying*, we all need to band together to find Psychic. In return for your help, I don't quite know what you get yet.'

Ace spoke. 'Can I hug him?'

'No.'

'Kiss him?'

'No!'

'Snog him?'

'Ace...'

'Can I sleep with him?'

'ACE!' Jaguar roared, jumping up from her seat! Ace smirked, annoyingly.

'Well then, what *do* I get?'

An idea – an horrific idea - came to Jaguar. She pondered it for a moment. Then, she said, 'You get me. *After* I've got him back. A month after, I'll arrive at ASIMOV tower, where...' Jaguar trailed off, knowing that everybody could see where it was going. Ultra Violet touched her arm in consternation. Turning to look, Jaguar saw her friend shake her head urgently.

'It's the only way.' Jaguar whispered, as UV's face fell. She sat down again.

Smiling, Ace bobbed her pudgy head. 'Deal.'

Jaguar's stomach dropped to the centre of the Earth. Truthfully, she had been hoping Ace would have said no.

As the meeting continued, they plotted courses, decided who was to go where and when, agreed, disagreed, and found themselves getting continually uneasy as the hours went by. Eventually, the two groups disbanded, Hades with numerous burns on his thigh, Bugman playing with the ladybird he'd found crawling across the floor, and Jaguar with a heavy heart, but Eclipse with an even heavier conscience.

Even as the long days and sleepless nights turned into weeks; and the weeks turned into months, and the months turned into one long year, Jaguar never lost hope, even though for half of the year she was stuck at home. It was a long and treacherous wait, fraught with depression, excitement, and, ultimately, desolation...

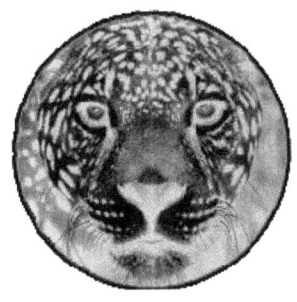

CHAPTER FIFTEEN

A year on…

Whirling snowflakes drifted down from the dark, cloudy sky, each one totally unique. They laid themselves to sleep on the already white-blanketed ground, melting into one thick layer of beautiful, treacherous cold. A short, black swathed figure ambled through the snow, looking out for any clues that might be helpful.

Six months ago, she had been heavily pregnant with triplets. Triplets that were now laid to rest, somewhere back in England, due to an ill-fated miscarriage. Sweet peas were sprinkled over the dug earth that now kept them safe from harm, in a small, beautiful graveyard. Now she was back on track with one goal in her mind - get Psychic back.

People milled about in front of gaily decorated shops, and she realised it was getting near Christmas. Robots, dollhouses, sweets, toys… Norway was beautiful in December. She couldn't understand Norwegian, and found herself wishing that she had a natural linguist with her. As it was, she was the only one in Norway. All the others had been sent to different locations around the world.

Jaguar didn't really expect to find Psychic here, but she liked the sights, the smells, and the feeling of such a gorgeous place.

Suddenly, Jaguar felt a pair of eyes on her. It was a sense she'd developed over the past year, for unknown reasons. Not much of a sixth sense, but it really did help. She whirled around, her warm cloak spraying snow everywhere as it fanned out around her.

The pair of eyes belonged to a man in a beige hat and long beige coat. She scrutinised him, then began to walk towards him. He immediately turned on his heel, and began striding away.

He knows something... Jaguar thought, quickening her pace. The anonymous man began to run; Jaguar's heart beat faster as she, too, went full speed. She could catch him up easily. Flurries of snow were thrown up every time one of her feet left the ground; her weight caused her to make heavy impressions in the snow. He turned a corner, as she hit 40mph. The distance between them was closing rapidly now (45, 47, 50!), until, ultimately, she leapt on his back, and down they went in a big puff of snow and ice.

Catching her breath, Jaguar realised she was lying on her back, with the man underneath her. Immediately, she changed her position so she was straddling him, and tore off his hat, which had miraculously managed to stay on his head. She unsheathed her claws while righting her mask, which was obscuring her vision of his face - and stopped dead.

Joy coursed through her veins, more than joy, even. She couldn't think of a word to describe her bliss. Jaguar threw her arms around Psychic, feeling that Heaven was a place on Earth.

He let her hold him tight for a bit, then said, 'Good to see you too, Jaguar. I really wish you weren't this obsessive, though.'

She stared down at him; then tugged off her mask. 'Psychic, is it me, or are you *looking* older?'

He gazed back at her. 'Sorry. I enabled my aging again. You shouldn't have come for me.'

'Why?'

'The children are in jeopardy!'

Taking a deep breath, Jaguar told him everything. Her eyes glistened as she recounted that fateful day. When she had ended, he looked like the end of the world had come about.

'I'm sorry, Hannah,' he said. It was the first time in a long while she had been called that.

'Dan…' She murmured back. Abruptly, he wriggled out from underneath her. Standing up, he opened his mouth to speak.

'I've got a new life here, Hannah. A home, friends…' he trailed off. She expected what was to come next.

Psychic continued sorrowfully. 'A new love.'

For poor Jaguar, she felt like Ace was ripping her bones apart, one by one. Her devastation was so immense; it was almost as if she was suddenly laid down by the weight of her bones. Her eyes met his, in a glance of pure horror.

'I guess I should move on, then,' she growled. She'd never expected to hate Psychic before, and it was a very instantaneous feeling. She slowly got up from the ground, dusting snow from her clothes. The cold began to bite at her.

'Maybe you should,' he told her.

Jaguar stepped forward and backhanded him across the cheek so hard, he fell sideways. Dan looked up at Hannah with hurt in his eyes, only to find that she was walking away.

What he didn't see were the tears rolling down her cheeks and joining the snow and ice on the ground.

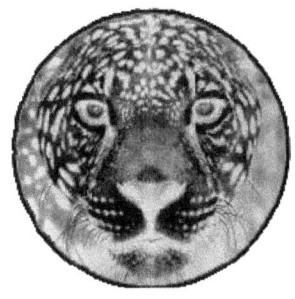

CHAPTER SIXTEEN

After the long, depressed journey home, Jaguar felt very tired. She'd been wearing the special clothes that UV and Flashe had worked together on to make for her. They shielded her metal.

Atom jumped around the corner, then, upon seeing Jaguar's expression, her puppy-dog face melted away, to be replaced with a look of confusion.

'Jag, why you sad? Have you gotted Psychic yeti?'

Jaguar stared at her, then understood that Atom was asking where Psychic was.

'He's not coming back,' Jaguar informed her, while preparing herself for the task of getting the word round to everyone to come back home.

~o0o~

Eventually, Phoenix returned from Canada, to find that Psychic was *not* back. Jaguar told her the story, and Phoenix couldn't believe it.

'But he loves you!' she protested.

'He used to. Now it's some other snotty Norwegian posh totty, I bet,' Jaguar spat.

After all the Demigods and their friends had returned to their rightful homes, it was time. Time for Jaguar to face her arch enemy - and at least *hope* to come out alive. Her heart was thumping as she got dressed that morning. Ultra Violet was staying on for a bit, and as Jaguar was about to open the door, UV crashed into her, sending them both toppling.

'Don't go, Jaguar! She'll kill you!' UV protested, desperately.

'I promised. I'm not really the kind to break my promises.'

'You promised you'd get Psychic back, and look what happened!'

At this, Jaguar's face went stony. 'Get out of my way, UV. You don't know just how dangerous I can be,' she growled. UV didn't move.

She really does care for me. Jaguar thought. It was nice of UV to try to stop her, but...

Jaguar stood up, disentangling herself from the distressed UV. UV was kneeling on the floor, her eyes brimming with tears. Jaguar turned her back and walked out, hopped on the quad and raced off.

~o0o~

UV understood now why ASIMOV didn't change their location. It was because ASIMOV would always win, in the end. The Demigods *did* have what they needed to defeat ASIMOV, which meant only one thing.

UV stood up, watching her small friend roar off into the night. She squared her shoulders and went to find Eclipse.

I swear to God Eclipse has something to do with this. UV thought.

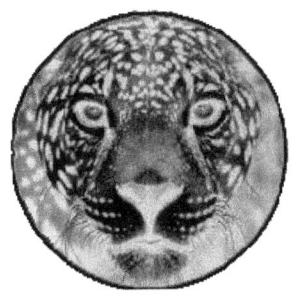

CHAPTER SEVENTEEN

ce stared out of the window. She knew Jaguar would come. The small thing never broke her promises, not intentionally. In due course, the red quad bike arrived in the grounds of the tower. Ace had stayed on the first floor that night, and so it only took her one flight of stairs to get to the ground floor. Her sister, Jack, had persuaded her to take the top floor in an effort for Ace to lose weight. Still, Ace always had a packet of *Hobnobs* in her desk drawer. She hadn't been *obese*, just a little bit pudgy, which was true. Over the past year, she had lost several stone, and was happy with her figure. Only 13 stone now! It was shaping up to be a *very* good Christmas indeed.

Ace opened the door wide. 'Jaguar! How nice of you to drop by!'

Jaguar pulled off her helmet. 'Enough of the pleasantries, Ace. Do what has to be done and get it over with.'

'With pleasure,' Ace smirked, evilly.

Jaguar marched across the sodden grass, only to be seized by four Jacks. Ace's heart fluttered with anticipation. The clones dragged Jaguar inside and down to the basement, which had been specially built for the Demigods. Ace saw Jaguar's head flick up at the sight of Maimai, unconscious and bleeding badly. Ace drew a mouldy curtain across Maimai's area. The clones shackled Jaguar to the wall. Ace stepped forward, tauntingly, and pulled off the mask on her old enemy's face. Burning blue eyes glared daggers at Ace.

'Hannah, you look very good. You haven't aged a bit!' Ace snorted.

~o0o~

Pain shot through Jaguar's left arm as Ace impaled it with something. But Jaguar had had worse, and so she stayed quiet. Something dripped on the floor, and Jaguar realised it was her own blood. Ace laughed.

All sorts of horrible instruments of torture awaited her, racked up on the walls. A scalpel, pistols, hacksaws, glass shards…was that a reverse bear trap? Ugh, she'd been watching too much *Saw*. Ace saw her looking at the hacksaws.

Jaguar decided she was in the presence of a homicidal maniac.

'Jaguar, where's your regular costume?' Ace asked.

'Didn't want to ruin it,' Jaguar snarled. She was in a red t-shirt and black jeans. Her trainers were black too; she'd had to keep the mask, though. It was important.

Ace pressed the hacksaw to Jaguar's thigh. 'Shall I, you stinking midget?' Ace snarled.

Jaguar felt sick. 'Whatever. I've got barely anything left anyway. The Demigods are drifting apart. UV seems a bit sick of me, even though she tried to stop me coming, and Eclipse is never there.'

Ace grinned. 'Then you shouldn't mind me doing *this!*' She dragged the thing sideways. Jaguar grunted, and Ace started to see metallic, shining bone.

'What *is* that colour, anyway?' Ace asked.

'Dunno. Take a picture; it'll last longer - oh, too late. Healed.'

Hades walked in: Jaguar's face darkened further.

'Wow. I knew you were Jaguar, but I didn't realise you were that geek girl at school. Hannah, right?'

Jaguar (or was she plain old Hannah Williams again?) said nothing. Her superhero title, it seemed, had been stripped from her.

'Can I help, boss?' Hades asked. Ace paused; then nodded.

Hannah Williams closed her eyes, taking deep, shuddering breaths. Ace clenched her hand into a ball, and Hannah screamed as her bones began moving.

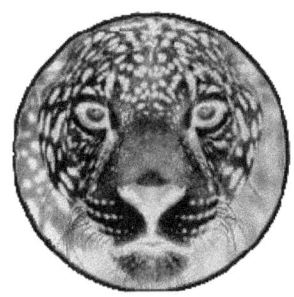

CHAPTER EIGHTEEN

P sychic sat alone on the hotel bed, brooding, just in jeans, no shirt. He didn't really have a new life. He didn't really have a new girl. All he knew was that his and Jaguar's marriage had been called off. No letters were sent out, but all the associates around the world he and the Demigods had shared, knew.

It felt weird, being single again, after... nine, ten years? It was like there was a Jaguar-shaped hole in his life. He could almost hear her calling his proper name.

DAN! PLEASE, DAN!

It rocked his head and he fell sideways on the bed. He jumped up and telepathically thought, as powerfully as he could, *JAGUAR? IS THAT YOU?*

A mental scream answered him, her scream. He knew that somewhere, somehow, she was in horrendous pain.

Psychic teleported to the source.

<poof>,

he was there. He found he was standing next to Maimai, who was severely hurt.

Quickly, he teleported her outside, next to …

Oh, no.

Next to Jaguar's quad bike.

Psychic sent a mental wave towards all the guards, who all collapsed. Psychic teleported back to where he just was; drew aside the curtain, to see another blood-splattered partition. A yell from it shook the building.

Her scream!

Psychic ripped the mouldy curtain aside so fiercely, it fell right off the rail. Ace and Hades turned around, with blood-soaked instruments in their blood-soaked hands. Jaguar, Hannah, *his* Hannah, was already healing. Her t-shirt was ripped around the bottom, but she still had her physical dignity. That was good.

Psychic stood there for a second, absolute wrath churning up instantly.

'Step... away... from... my... Jaguar,' he snarled. Hades jumped forwards and sliced him with a scalpel or something, Jaguar's blood mixing into his. Psychic telekinetically smashed Hades against the wall, and there was a sickening crack. To Psychic, it was the most glorious crack in the universe.

He turned his attention to Ace, who was standing there with a saw and a stake, or something, in her hands. Ace dropped them both, but it was too late. His hand wrapped around her pudgy neck, squeezing tighter and tighter. Ace choked and scrabbled at his hand.

'Super strength won't work for you now, will it?' he snarled, psychically reinforcing his grasp. He heard Jaguar saying, 'No, stop, wait. You don't understand...'

Psychic couldn't stop. He felt himself getting stronger and stronger, and using only his mind, smashed the wall apart, into another room. He flung Ace into it, and brought the ceiling crashing down on her. She didn't move again. He looked at Jaguar, who, even with tears and blood coating her face, looked achingly beautiful.

'I promised them that I would let them have me if I got you back,' Jaguar choked.

'You didn't get me back, though.'

'I knew you'd come, anyway. So if I hadn't come, I would have been breaking my promise...'

'You really need to let go of that,' Psychic smiled. Striding forwards, he telekinetically snapped the shackles and caught Jaguar as she slid down the wall. Exhausted, she gazed back at him, and dropped unconscious.

Once outside, Psychic noticed that both Maimai and the quad were gone. He didn't mind. He could fly Jaguar back. His wings burst out of his back, and, with several flaps, he lifted off. It was just beginning to rain, and it landed on Jaguar's red-smeared forehead. Just this once, he looked into her mind.

...not jaguar, Hannah
does he still love me
it hurt so much
I'm Hannah not jaguar
i don't deserve to be jaguar
not good enough
He's in my head
love you
don't be in my head though
Jesus
Dammit, get out of my head
Psychic, please get out of my head.

Her eyes fluttered open, to meet his, with a look of knowing.

'When you're in my mind, I can sort of see in yours,' she told him.

'And then..?' Psychic asked.

She punched him on the shoulder. 'You liar! You don't have a new girlfriend! And may I add, you really *do* need a life…'

Psychic smirked. 'Oh, be quiet.'

'Psychic- Dan. Dan, why did you say those things to me?'

'Ask Ace. Well, ask her dead body.'

'Tell me.'

So Psychic told Jaguar.

He told her about how ASIMOV had threatened to kill Jaguar and the unborn children if he didn't do as commanded. They'd known because of a new ASIMOV, Infra-Red, who saw in heat vision only. He had seen the new lives growing inside of Jaguar, and reported back instantly. Therefore, Ace had come up with a plan to ruin the Demigods forever. When Jaguar had told Psychic of the miscarriage, Psychic had instantly started to rebel.

'What I don't understand, though,' Jaguar told him, as they were flying over the Thames, 'is how the kids actually, um…' She stopped there, feeling awkward. Psychic felt it too.

'I know. It's like in Star Wars, where Anakin was just randomly born without a dad.'

'Psychic, Star Wars isn't real.'

'Well, how about that urban legend you told me once, where this guy gets shot in the, um… dude area, and the bullet hits this girl?'

'Psychic, that's an *urban legend*. And I don't recall you getting shot in the 'dude area' and then me getting the bullet.'

'Well… I don't know. Let's just leave it at the Star Wars explanation then.'

'Yes please.'

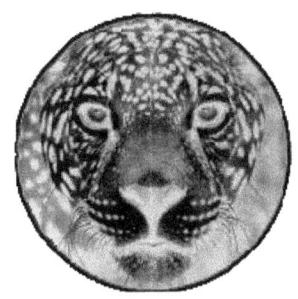

CHAPTER NINETEEN

Atom didn't want to go home, even when everyone had stopped searching for Sicic. She found it really fun to run around the house a lot! So when Sicic landed in the garden, in the pouring rain, with Jaggy in his arms, Atom's logic had told her that something was wrong.

'Sicic, whassup? Has Jaggy been playing wiv the wed food colouring again?'

'Jaguar's hurt, Atom.'

'No, I'm not!' Jaguar protested. Atom was confused.

'Well, is she hurt or not?' Atom asked.

Sicic disappeared and Atom decided not to worry about it.

~o0o~

UV screamed momentarily, before Eclipse clapped her hand over UV's mouth.

'What do you *think* I am, a traitor?' Eclipse hissed. UV bit Eclipse's hand, viciously. Eclipse ignored it and pushed UV up against the wall, before getting out her gun.

I was saving this for you, Jaguar, in times of desperate need, but... Eclipse jammed the gun under UV's jaw and clicked back the safety.

'Do you think I would *ever* betray them like that, huh? Jaguar's one of my closest friends!' Eclipse growled.

She froze. UV looked at her, questioningly. Eclipse looked at the door, then at UV. 'You dare try to tell them I'm with ASIMOV and I'll goddamn shoot you. That would be a lie, and you don't like lying, do you?'

UV glared at her. Eclipse backed off immediately, holstered the pistol, and fixed a friendly smile on her face.

'What the?' spluttered UV, before Psychic burst into the hallway and down the basement to Flashe's lab. UV stared after him, then broke into a run and followed. Psychic smashed down the door, and Eclipse realised he had no top on. A disgusted shiver ran down her spine.

Ew. Topless Psychic. Not nice at all. She thought.

~oOo~

Flashe looked up to see Psychic in the doorway, with Jaguar looking thoroughly injured. Her hand flew to her mouth and she cleared everything off the table. Glasses smashed and acid burnt the floor, but right now her friend needed her help. Flashe tugged off her rubber gloves and pulled on new ones. She shooed everyone out, but Psychic stayed. Flashe looked him in the eye.

'You do realise that ...'

'I won't look at her!'

Flashe nodded and cut open Jaguar's top. Jaguar had evidently fallen back into unconsciousness. Flashe could see little bumps randomly strewn across the front, and realised that Jaguar must have gone to Ace. Oh, the stupid woman! Flashe scrutinised the bumps, and realised that they were lead bullets.

They must have been fired at point-blank range to not have been expelled by Jaguar's healing power.

She thought quickly, her scientific mind running through lots of different possibilities. Flashe fished a scalpel out from the wall rack and, gritting her teeth, began extracting the bullets. Jaguar started moaning in her sleep for Psychic, and Flashe took her hand and placed it in Psychic's. He had his eyes closed, not wanting to see anything. His hand gripped hers tightly, and she stopped muttering.

Flashe stood back, finished at last. 'Don't open your eyes yet, Psychic. She's still, uh…'

'I understand.'

'Do you want a top or something? You don't have one on.'

'I think *she's* more important than a top for me right now.'

'Yeah. Yeah, okay'.

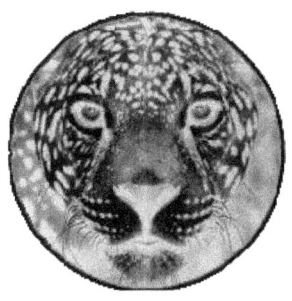

CHAPTER TWENTY

Phoenix nudged the door open with her shoulder. Jaguar was still asleep, in bed. The tray Phoenix was holding wobbled slightly as she placed it on the bedside table.

'There you go, Psychic. Redbush tea, cookies…,' she stopped. He knew already. Of course he knew. She felt left out. Psychic didn't look up. Instead he stroked his lover's hand. She sighed.

Just as Phoenix was about to leave the room, however, Jaguar sat bolt upright and gasped, 'Phoenix, don't you dare bloody leave this room unless I say so.'

Phoenix whirled around, grinning. Her friend was back, and better than ever. Jaguar caught her eye and smiled. Phoenix gestured to the tray. 'I brought stuff…'

Jaguar looked, reached for a cookie, and jammed it into her mouth. 'Mfg fghmfhf!' She mumbled, through a mouthful of crumbs. Phoenix raised an eyebrow. Jaguar swallowed, and tried again.

'I'm back!' Jaguar crowed, triumphantly. Phoenix and Psychic laughed and laughed.

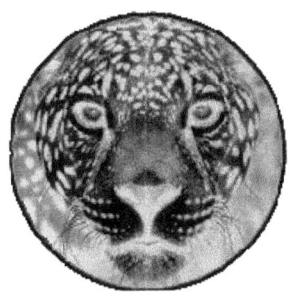

CHAPTER TWENTY-ONE

Wondering if she should come up with a new name for herself, Jack filed away at her nails in her study. Ace had been right (before Psychic killed her); people were getting confused about her gender. Something to do with card packs, maybe? It was all getting a bit weird.

Hyper appeared in front of the desk. Jack jumped, startled.

'What?' She blurted out. Hyper's eyes were different. They were red, with a sort of black, cat pupil slit in the middle. Jack narrowed her own eyes, before she was cast back against the wall by pure energy. She couldn't move.

'I have a bone to pick with Ace. Several, actually,' he snarled. Jack couldn't breathe as he stalked closer. His forearm pressed against her throat, contracting her airway.

'Ace-Ace--gkk—is dead-,' Jack choked out. Hyper nodded.

'Thought so. Well, I'm going to destroy this tower so I suggest you run.'

With that, Hyper *bamf*-ed somewhere else, and Jack heard muffled BOOMs from the foundations. She hit the panic button under her desk and yelled into the microphone, 'EVERYBODY OUT! I REPEAT, OUT! GET OUT OF THE TOWER!' Jack herself then turned tail and ran like the wind down the steps. She didn't stop for breath once.

Finally, she made it to the front door and pelted out. A lot of other members were there too, running for their lives. Nobody could stop Hyper. She kept running. There was an almighty explosion and rubble was cast into the air. Suddenly Jack saw a shadow in front of her; it was the tower, the tower was falling and she thought for a moment…

If I knew I wasn't going to die here, what part of the card deck would *my name have been?*

All of a sudden, something hit Jack's head very hard and she knew no more.

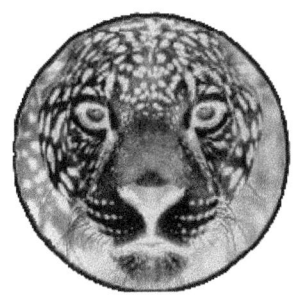

CHAPTER TWENTY-TWO

A rrow turned on the TV, and switched to the news. Images flashed up of wars and stuff, and he settled down to watch it with a bowl of sushi. Spontaneously, he jumped - spilling fish everywhere - as footage of ASIMOV tower collapsing appeared on the screen. He grinned hugely. Captured on camera was Hyper, blasting at the tower with unalloyed energy. His face was too blurred to make out his features, but Arrow guessed that Hyper would be on the run for a while after this.

The camera zoomed into a clip of Jack, running into the forest, looking ever so bewildered. Arrow assumed that she was scared and alone. Good!

~o0o~

She had no idea who she was, or what had just happened. All she knew was that she had to run, and that she had to choose a number between two and ten.

All she knew was that Night fell, and she got cold.

Suddenly, a pair of scary eyes appeared in front of her. She yelped. She'd seen red eyes before, but these were different. Several forms dropped down from the trees.

Seven of them.

Seven.

Seven. She thought. *I am Seven.*

The shapes began to walk around her and she realised she could make copies of herself.

Instantaneously, twelve of her appeared; all holding knives, exactly like she was.

Attack. She thought. All of her, including Seven herself, spun into action, defeating the things. She realised, as the last one fell, that they were vampires.

Seven decided that vampires were very bad. She also decided to change what she looked like, just in case anyone tried to find her. These powers were... breath-taking. For some reason, she wasn't scared that she had them. She just knew that she was a superhuman, and accepted it with tranquillity.

Her long, blonde hair instantly became black, and her pale skin turned tan. She found she didn't need her glasses any more, and crushed them under her foot.

Seven squared her shoulders and walked off, while her clones disappeared, to find more vampires. She knew they were immortal. She knew a lot of immortal people. Demigods? And the Demigods' friends, too. There was one in particular... Puma?

Leopard?

No.

Jaguar.

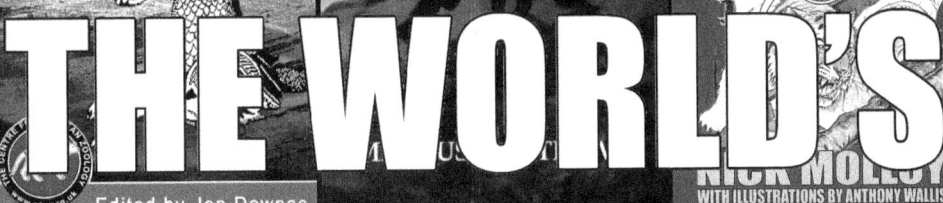

HOW TO START A PUBLISHING EMPIRE

Unlike most mainstream publishers, we have a non-commercial remit, and our mission statement claims that "we publish books because they deserve to be published, not because we think that we can make money out of them". Our motto is the Latin Tag *Pro bona causa facimus* (we do it for good reason), a slogan taken from a children's book *The Case of the Silver Egg* by the late Desmond Skirrow.

WIKIPEDIA: "The first book published was in 1988. *Take this Brother may it Serve you Well* was a guide to Beatles bootlegs by Jonathan Downes. It sold quite well, but was hampered by very poor production values, being photocopied, and held together by a plastic clip binder. In 1988 A5 clip binders were hard to get hold of, so the publishers took A4 binders and cut them in half with a hacksaw. It now reaches surprisingly high prices second hand.

The production quality improved slightly over the years, and after 1999 all the books produced were ringbound with laminated colour covers. In 2004, however, they signed an agreement with Lightning Source, and all books are now produced perfect bound, with full colour covers."

Until 2010 all our books, the majority of which are/were on the subject of mystery animals and allied disciplines, were published by `CFZ Press`, the publishing arm of the Centre for Fortean Zoology (CFZ), and we urged our readers and followers to draw a discreet veil over the books that we published that were completely off topic to the CFZ.

However, in 2010 we decided that enough was enough and launched a second imprint, `Fortean Words` which aims to cover a wide range of non animal-related esoteric subjects. Other imprints will be launched as and when we feel like it, however the basic ethos of the company remains the same: Our job is to publish books and magazines that we feel are worth publishing, whether or not they are going to sell. Money is, after all - as my dear old Mama once told me - a rather vulgar subject, and she would be rolling in her grave if she thought that her eldest son was somehow in `trade`.

Luckily, so far our tastes have turned out not to be that rarified after all, and we have sold far more books than anyone ever thought that we would, so there is a moral in there somewhere…

Jon Downes,
Woolsery, North Devon
July 2010

CFZ PRESS

Other Books in Print

ORANG PENDEK: Sumatra's Forgotten Ape by Richard Freeman
THE MYSTERY ANIMALS OF THE BRITISH ISLES: London by Neil Arnold
CFZ EXPEDITION REPORT: India 2010 by Richard Freeman *et al*
The Cryptid Creatures of Florida by Scott Marlow
Dead of Night by Lee Walker
The Mystery Animals of the British Isles: The Northern Isles by Glen Vaudrey
THE MYSTERY ANIMALS OF THE BRTISH ISLES: Gloucestershire and Worcestershire by
Paul Williams
When Bigfoot Attacks by Michael Newton
Weird Waters – The Mystery Animals of Scandinavia: Lake and Sea Monsters by Lars Thomas
The Inhumanoids by Barton Nunnelly
Monstrum! A Wizard's Tale by Tony "Doc" Shiels
CFZ Yearbook 2011 edited by Jonathan Downes
Karl Shuker's Alien Zoo by Shuker, Dr Karl P.N
Tetrapod Zoology Book One by Naish, Dr Darren
The Mystery Animals of Ireland by Gary Cunningham and Ronan Coghlan
Monsters of Texas by Gerhard, Ken
The Great Yokai Encyclopaedia by Freeman, Richard
NEW HORIZONS: Animals & Men *issues 16-20 Collected Editions Vol. 4*
by Downes, Jonathan
A Daintree Diary -
Tales from Travels to the Daintree Rainforest in tropical north Queensland, Australia
by Portman, Carl
Strangely Strange but Oddly Normal by Roberts, Andy
Centre for Fortean Zoology Yearbook 2010 by Downes, Jonathan
Predator Deathmatch by Molloy, Nick
Star Steeds and other Dreams by Shuker, Karl
CHINA: A Yellow Peril? by Muirhead, Richard
Mystery Animals of the British Isles: The Western Isles by Vaudrey, Glen

Giant Snakes - Unravelling the coils of mystery by Newton, Michael
Mystery Animals of the British Isles: Kent by Arnold, Neil
Centre for Fortean Zoology Yearbook 2009 by Downes, Jonathan
CFZ EXPEDITION REPORT: Russia 2008 by Richard Freeman *et al*, Shuker, Karl (fwd)
Dinosaurs and other Prehistoric Animals on Stamps - A Worldwide catalogue
by Shuker, Karl P. N
Dr Shuker's Casebook by Shuker, Karl P.N
The Island of Paradise - chupacabra UFO crash retrievals,
and accelerated evolution on the island of Puerto Rico by Downes, Jonathan
The Mystery Animals of the British Isles: Northumberland and Tyneside by Hallowell, Michael J
Centre for Fortean Zoology Yearbook 1997 by Downes, Jonathan (Ed)
Centre for Fortean Zoology Yearbook 2002 by Downes, Jonathan (Ed)
Centre for Fortean Zoology Yearbook 2000/1 by Downes, Jonathan (Ed)
Centre for Fortean Zoology Yearbook 1998 by Downes, Jonathan (Ed)
Centre for Fortean Zoology Yearbook 2003 by Downes, Jonathan (Ed)
In the wake of Bernard Heuvelmans by Woodley, Michael A
CFZ EXPEDITION REPORT: Guyana 2007 by Richard Freeman *et al*, Shuker, Karl (fwd)
Centre for Fortean Zoology Yearbook 1999 by Downes, Jonathan (Ed)
Big Cats in Britain Yearbook 2008 by Fraser, Mark (Ed)
Centre for Fortean Zoology Yearbook 1996 by Downes, Jonathan (Ed)
THE CALL OF THE WILD - Animals & Men issues 11-15
Collected Editions Vol. 3 by Downes, Jonathan (ed)
Ethna's Journal by Downes, C N
Centre for Fortean Zoology Yearbook 2008 by Downes, J (Ed)
DARK DORSET -Calendar Custome by Newland, Robert J
Extraordinary Animals Revisited by Shuker, Karl
MAN-MONKEY - In Search of the British Bigfoot by Redfern, Nick
Dark Dorset Tales of Mystery, Wonder and Terror by Newland, Robert J and Mark North
Big Cats Loose in Britain by Matthews, Marcus
MONSTER! - The A-Z of Zooform Phenomena by Arnold, Neil
The Centre for Fortean Zoology 2004 Yearbook by Downes, Jonathan (Ed)
The Centre for Fortean Zoology 2007 Yearbook by Downes, Jonathan (Ed)
CAT FLAPS! Northern Mystery Cats by Roberts, Andy
Big Cats in Britain Yearbook 2007 by Fraser, Mark (Ed)
BIG BIRD! - Modern sightings of Flying Monsters by Gerhard, Ken
THE NUMBER OF THE BEAST - Animals & Men issues 6-10
Collected Editions Vol. 1 by Downes, Jonathan (Ed)
IN THE BEGINNING - Animals & Men *issues 1-5 Collected Editions Vol. 1* by Downes, Jonathan
STRENGTH THROUGH KOI - They saved Hitler's Koi and other stories
by Downes, Jonathan
The Smaller Mystery Carnivores of the Westcountry by Downes, Jonathan
CFZ EXPEDITION REPORT: Gambia 2006 by Richard Freeman *et al*, Shuker, Karl (fwd)
The Owlman and Others by Jonathan Downes
The Blackdown Mystery by Downes, Jonathan

Big Cats in Britain Yearbook 2006 by Fraser, Mark (Ed)
Fragrant Harbours - Distant Rivers by Downes, John T
Only Fools and Goatsuckers by Downes, Jonathan
Monster of the Mere by Jonathan Downes
Dragons:More than a Myth by Freeman, Richard Alan
Granfer's Bible Stories by Downes, John Tweddell
Monster Hunter by Downes, Jonathan

Fortean Words

The Centre for Fortean Zoology has for several years led the field in Fortean publishing. CFZ Press is the only publishing company specialising in books on monsters and mystery animals. CFZ Press has published more books on this subject than any other company in history and has attracted such well known authors as Andy Roberts, Nick Redfern, Michael Newton, Dr Karl Shuker, Neil Arnold, Dr Darren Naish, Jon Downes, Ken Gerhard and Richard Freeman.

Now CFZ Press are launching a new imprint. Fortean Words is a new line of books dealing with Fortean subjects other than cryptozoology, which is - after all - the subject the CFZ are best known for. Fortean Words is being launched with a spectacular multi-volume series called *Haunted Skies* which covers British UFO sightings between 1940 and 2010. Former policeman John Hanson and his long-suffering partner Dawn Holloway have compiled a peerless library of sighting reports, many that have not been made public before.

Other books include a look at the Berwyn Mountains UFO case by renowned Fortean Andy Roberts and a series of forthcoming books by transatlantic researcher Nick Redfern. CFZ Press are dedicated to maintaining the fine quality of their works with Fortean Words. New authors tackling new subjects will always be encouraged, and we hope that our books will continue to be as ground-breaking and popular as ever.

Haunted Skies Volume One 1940-1959 by John Hanson and Dawn Holloway
Haunted Skies Volume Two 1960-1965 by John Hanson and Dawn Holloway
Haunted Skies Volume Three 1965-1967 by John Hanson and Dawn Holloway
Haunted Skies Volume Four 1968-1971 by John Hanson and Dawn Holloway
Grave Concerns by Kai Roberts

Police and the Paranormal by Andy Owens
Dead of Night by Lee Walker
Space Girl Dead on Spaghetti Junction - an anthology by Nick Redfern
I Fort the Lore - an anthology by Paul Screeton
UFO Down - the Berwyn Mountains UFO Crash by Andy Roberts

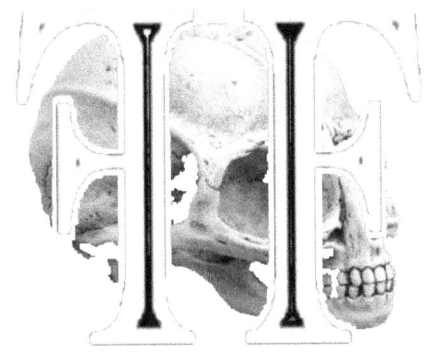

Fortean Fiction

J ust before Christmas 2011, we launched our third imprint, this time dedicated to - let's see if you guessed it from the title - fictional books with a Fortean or cryptozoological theme. We have published a few fictional books in the past, but now think that because of our rising reputation as publishers of quality Forteana, that a dedicated fiction imprint was the order of the day.

We launched with four titles:

Green Unpleasant Land by Richard Freeman
Left Behind by Harriet Wadham
Dark Ness by Tabitca Cope
Snap! By Steven Bredice